Author/CEO Darrell King

COO/Marketing Mngr. Elbert Jones Jr.

KJ Publications, Inc.

www.kjpublications.com

"The Evolution Of Street"

Chapter One

The 54 years old Ellen Marshall was walking out of the five bedroom duplex she shared with her husband and four kids, carrying the blue Mulberry Bayswater she got from a fashion store she visited last week. Her matching blue suit and black suede skirt stood firm on her body as she opened the back door of her car and dropped the light bag on the chair. She walked to the other side of the car and got into the driver's seat.

The time was still six minutes before seven but she was not the type who would wait till she had to rush to get to work. So she always left home five minutes before seven so that she could make the twenty-five minutes' drive to her workplace, with enough time to rest her head and start the day's work.

As she had supposed, she got to her work place some minutes before most of her colleagues would arrive, she used that opportunity to take a quick bite out of her breakfast of toast bread and veggies, and within the twenty minutes before she resumed duty, she was able to consume everything she had carried along.

"Hey Ellen!" one of her few coworkers who always managed to make it to the office some few minutes before eight greeted her. She had just gotten down from her own car and walked up to Ellen's. Maggie had always been that way with Ellen - ever since she started the job about four years back. Maggie knew that Ellen would always have her breakfast in her car before it was time for their daily tasks to begin and if she could manage, Ellen would still try to do some office work before getting into the actual office.

"Maggie. How are you doing?" she smiled at the other woman out of the necessity of not portraying herself as a bitch - but if left to her, she really didn't care for what people thought of her - she had better things to worry about.

"As always Ellen." Maggie answered. Maggie had dubbed the 'as always' reply since she found that trying to answer Ellen in a particular way that provided either too much or too little information did nothing to improve the impression the woman already had about her. And as usual, Ellen only nodded to her reply and went to clearing the crumbs that had fallen while she was eating and the little coffee she had spilled when she wanted to open the cup. She had bought herself disposable coffee cups so that she didn't have to go to any of the Starbucks shop along her way - she preferred having coffee she brewed by herself. "You know I've not forgotten about the dinner we have been planning for some time now." Maggie chipped in like she always did every morning.

When Maggie started her job at the agency four years ago, Ellen had been happy to have a fellow black woman to talk with but all her enthusiasm died when she got to know that Maggie favored democrats. Maggie had even told her that her mother had raised her on welfare and that had sealed her decision to keep the woman at arms' length. She had made the mistake of inviting the woman and her family on her first day at work to dinner at her house - but once she knew everything about her upbringing and political inclination, she had made sure that the dinner never became a reality and still making sure it stays that way.

"I've not found the right moment for the dinner Maggie. You know I don't just do things that would later come out to be imperfect. I need to make sure that whatever time we would have the dinner would be the best it could be." Ellen said as she managed to look at the woman this time around.

"I know you'll still find a time for us to hang out Ellen." Maggie smiled at Ellen and walked towards the entrance to the building. Ellen could have done what she usually did with everyone she didn't like - tell them outright that she was never going to be friends with them, but with Maggie, things were different. Although they were both black, she figured that Maggie would have lots of rejection while she was growing up because her self-esteem was totally drained, and she wouldn't be a good person if she worsened that situation by also refusing to relate with the woman. She could not even begin to imagine what her kids would be like - when they had to see a mother who does not believe in herself and would always want the approval of others. She had let the woman keep talking to her and she replied as polite as she could without having to discuss anything with her or prolong their dialogue for more than few minutes. She knew that she would finally have to deal with Maggie's case the way she did others' but that day was not today - she had better things to do with her time. She would just ignore Maggie for the rest of the day as she has always done for the years she's been working at the agency.

By the time Ellen Marshall got out of her car and walked into the office, it was just a minute before eight and at that time, every other agent began to walk in briskly through the front door - each one of them heading to their allocated space in the building along Tyvola Drive, Charlotte, North Carolina. It was time to leave behind the world outside and face her job - a job that she was always happy to do. She had the opportunity to always make sure that her people - though she would never agree that they are her people - she would make sure that they did not get what their lazy ass was always fighting to get - entry into her great country - it was meant for people like her.

Chapter Two

Juanita Lopez had been home all day. She was just recovering from the flu she had been battling for days. She wanted to make sure that she was fully okay before she resumed going for lectures again. Her roommates and friends have made sure that she didn't miss out on any assignments sob far and luckily for her, they haven't done any test - so she had been safe sitting at home all the while. Every Tuesday, she was meant to have lectures till late into the evening so her roommates were not home yet when she got the usual knock on the door to the flat they were staying. She knew that the only people who could be knocking on the door at past four in the afternoon were the kids from the house opposite their apartment - and surely they were the ones she met standing with expectant eyes when she opened the door.

"Hey kidos." She yelled with excitement. She would have preferred if she could have had the evening to herself before her friends made it back from class, yet she could not deny that having the children around the house made her feel good a bit - somewhat responsible.

"Hello Anita." They echoed and murmured her name as they filed into the flat. The seventeen squared meter living room and study still contained little furniture. They only had two small cushions and a table with a chair at one end for studying. She had moved the love seat that used to sit next to one of the cushions to her room when her boyfriend was staying over often - he was practically living with them at that time.

"Latifah and Laura are not back yet?" Tanya asked.

Tanya was the first daughter of her neighbor and she had been the first to start the visit before her younger ones joined her. "They should be home any moment from now." Juanita answered.

"So you're not feeling so fine yet." David commented as he went through their bookshelf that stood at one end of the living room. He was always rummaging through the sweet smelling wooden box that carried the books the ladies read. They didn't get to add new books frequently so she was not sure why David always went through it - he should already know that it was the same book that has been on it two months ago that was still on it.

"I think I'm better. I just don't feel like going back to class yet. Maybe by next week." Juanita answered the boy's question as she moved around to make sure that the little kids were not sauntering into where they were not supposed to. "Your mum isn't back from work yet?" she asked although she already knew the answer.

"You know my mum - she's a workaholic. I'm sure that she wouldn't mind going to work on every public holiday." Tanya joked lightly before she answered the question seriously. "She called me a few minutes ago and said she was going to be stopping in some grocery store to shop a bit."

"Alright." Juanita said briefly. Mrs. Marshall had made it known that she didn't like her kids coming around to their house but since the kids didn't feel like they could manage always been in their home alone after school till when their mother arrived home late in the evening; they didn't give much heed to what their mother had said. The only thing Juanita could do now was to make sure that Ellen didn't pop up suddenly and catch her kids in the flat - she knew there would be trouble if that happened, and none of them wanted that. "But then you guys can't stay long. I don't want any trouble with your mum." She added. The kids couldn't still understand why they were not allowed to play with anybody else in the neighborhood. They only made friends with few kids - the ones their parents wanted them to hang out with.

"We know Anita. We just couldn't sit at home till our mum gets home." David said. "You still got that Tom Clancy book?" he asked. He had not stopped looking through the shelf since he got inside.

"There are lots of Tom Clancy on that shelf. Which one are you talking about exactly?" Juanita asked.

"Well, that's the problem. I don't really remember the title - it's been a while since I read it." David answered.

"I can't help you then. Maybe you'll just keep looking till you find what you are looking for."

"Nah. I cannot go through all these books before my mum gets back and who the hell knows when we would be able to come out like this again." He complained.

"You shouldn't forget the stories you read David - how can you forget stories? No one does that!" Juanita yelled lovingly at the boy who was already looking disappointed. "I'll keep it for you if I come across it anytime." She promised hoping that would lighten up his mood - and it sure did.

"We haven't seen Richard here for quite some time. Are you guys still good?" Tanya imposed.

She didn't feel like answering that question but she knew that the girl meant no harm when she asked and if she decided not to answer, who knows what that might stir up in her. "Sure. We are good. We're just taking things easy these days. You would understand everything when you grow up and begin to have boyfriends." Juanita answered without revealing much details. "You guys need to be back in the house now. Your mum would be home any minute from now and I don't want any trouble." Juanita said to the kids who were beginning to settle down into the house. They always felt at home on the cushion and even though she wished she could have more of them around her, she couldn't think of how to deal with their mother - she was a total bitch, something she would have gotten from all the years of being married to her husband.

"Yeah we know." Tanya said, her head hanging droopingly. "Come on. Let's get home now." She said to her siblings and they filed out of the apartment, crossed the street and got into their house.

Chapter Three

"You gonna get us something to eat or not?" Latifah who was seating on one of the couches asked Juanita.

"And why do I have to get you younginz what you're going to eat? Don't you both know how to cook?" Juanita replied.

"Well, you've been home all day so you should have done at least that. It isn't like you're not feeling good again." Latifah answered. "Moreover, you cook good food - not that it's better than what I make, but you sure know how to cook better than Laura. You're not good for nothing." She added to tease her quiet friend.

"Nah. She's ain't not good for nothing. She's good for fucking - and sucking too. The way she deep throats that her guy, I'm sure that her saliva would forever be all over his dick." Laura joined in the game.

"You girls think I'm going to say something to all these bullshit?" Juanita spoke up. She knew what they were doing and she wasn't going to let herself be a victim. "I'm gonna go into my room now and when either you or Laura have prepared the food, I'll come out to eat." She announced and walked out of the room leaving both Laura and Latifah in a fit of laughter.

"Hey. You all should go to bed now. It's getting late." Ellen Marshall said to her kids who were watching TV in the living room. "I don't know why you kids always wait for me to chase you to your rooms before you go to bed." She murmured under her breath.

She had arrived home late in the evening and she was just getting to rest since arriving home. Her husband had also arrived few minutes after her and he has been busy in their bedroom since then. He was the managing director of an advertising company. He had started the company right after leaving college with two of his buddies and for the past seven years, the company has started receiving big jobs from notable clients - everything with the business was always getting better which meant that he had to put in more hours every day to make sure that they didn't fail any of their clients.

Ellen sat in the living room for a while before she walked back to her husband in the bedroom - it was getting late and she needed a lot of rest.

Chapter Four

It was fast approaching summer but the girls had no intention of going to be with family. They wanted to spend summer in school so they were in no hurry to pack their belongings when others were. Ellen Marshall had noticed this and she was worried. She didn't have the stomach to put up with the girls any longer, not that they did anything that directly concerns her but all what they stood for was against her belief and principles. She could not understand how they would believe that the world should be made in a way that would be fair for everyone. The world had never been fair, not before they were born, not during all the years they've been alive and it would never be. It was just that way and she couldn't comprehend why they were trying to fight it - as though they were God.

She could have managed to have the girls in the neighborhood, at least, they've been staying there for more than a year and the only heated moment she'd had with them so far was just yelling. But now, it seemed like they had their partners with them. She was going to give them a piece of herself but not tonight, she decided and left the window where she had been standing for close to thirty minutes.

"You know it's just gonna be better if we can find a way to make sure that they leave this community. Those girls are just bunch o' nuisance." Her husband Roy spoke up.

"You think they don't know we tryna kick 'em outta our hood?" Ellen answered her husband's unasked question. "They're making sure that they don't do anything that can help us with that fight."

"Maybe we should just kick 'em out then. Rather than looking for some ways that might not work. We could just buy the house and tell them to move out that it needs some renovation. That would work." Roy suggested.

Ellen looked at her husband for a while before she spoke. "It cannot work. I have already tried it." she replied curtly.

"What do you mean by that? How would you know?" Roy asked his wife. Sometimes he was not sure he knew who he had married, but he always loved her more because of that - the mystery.

"I've spoken to the owner of the house and I offered him a hundred grand just to get that building and he wouldn't agree. I even promised him that would be the first instalment for the payment and that I was gonna be giving him another hundred grand after I get the house but he refused. He was saying some shit about it being the most precious thing to him and no price can make him give it up." Ellen explained herself.

"You already spoke to the landlord?" he asked, though he was not too shocked.

"Well, I wanted to have something tangible before I brought the idea to you and since the man didn't agree to the deal I didn't see any reason to tell you 'bout it – it's one of the million things I've tried to use to get them out of the neighborhood." Ella added.

"We gonna get them babe – one way or the other. You don't need to worry."

"It's the kids I worry for. They don't realize that what those girls are preaching isn't healthy for the society. Tanya believes that they are just friendly and it wouldn't be nice not to return that. She does not know that those are all strategies to convince them that everyone can be cool with each other - and it would work if we don't do something about it fast." Ella complained.

"We gonna be having a new president soon that would favor our policies and principles and by then those girls would see what being free really means." Roy replied. "The kids will be with your mum for most of the break so don't worry about them." He added.

He pulled her away from the curtain where she had been standing after turning away from the window and sat her on his laps. "We all know that people like those girls are gonna try their best to make sure that our guy doesn't get in but we know our way around things than they so we would come out victorious in that battle. And you know if that happens, things are gonna favor us. So we just do the shit we know how to do best and make sure those assholes don't get nowhere near us." He completed his statement and didn't wait for his wife to reply before digging his hands into the blouse of her gown, cupping her breast in his hands and his other hand feeling her up from beneath.

She was still as young as she was from the first day he had met her. She went to the gym twice a week to make sure there were no fat in any part of her body. She had no time for tanning herself - like she needed it. She was usually considered a white black woman by most people she had gotten acquainted with - not just because she was light skinned, but also because of her idealism. They in no way proclaimed what majority of the black people want with life, if he was allowed to speak his mind.

Her parents had instilled the values of a true Republican in her and she had grown to love it. It had been something she could have walked away from as she grew but she chose instead to stay with it because it made her fulfilled and it was the only thing that she believed could keep the world balance.

She had great vigor fighting for what she believed in and he knew that if he let her handle their neighbors' case alone, she would find a way to get them out, and it wouldn't be just out of their neighborhood, she would make sure that had a first hand of what hell on earth means.

As he kept savoring the youthfulness of his wife from head to toe, all these thoughts came to him and he loved her even more. She was really the bone of his bone and flesh of his flesh.

Chapter Five

Latifah Muhammad was in her room, alone with her boyfriend Josh. It was already night and everyone was sapped. They had partied all day on their lawn. A few friends were around for the party but now, everywhere was quiet once again. Josh had left the party earlier than the rest of them and he was already asleep on the bed. She knew that he was tired to do anything else that night, and she was supposed to try to get a good night rest also but she just couldn't. She had been thinking all day about how she would want him inside of her tonight and if she didn't satisfy the hunger that she was battling before falling asleep, the next day would be hell for both of them - they would not get out of bed the whole day.

"Hey baby..." she called him in a soothing voice and began to rouse him from his sleep. "Wake up Josh..." she called him when he didn't want to stand up from the bed.

"What is it?" Josh murmured but didn't raise his head from the pillow.

"Just stand up for a while uh....." she drawled into his ear and kept humming irritating sounds into his ear until he had no choice but to obey.

"Why won't you let me sleep Latifah? I'm very tired right now." Josh complained but his girlfriend had no ear for that.

"I'll let you sleep back baby but I need you right now." Latifah smiled at him when he shook his head at her announcement.

"You wake me up just because you want us to fuck? Come on Tipha, we can do this tomorrow morning. You got no class to worry about." Josh replied her.

"I'm horny right now Josh. I can't wait till tomorrow morning. I need you inside of me tonight." Latifah protested.

"If you're horny, I know you've got some dildos around. Just use it and if you don't have, you can meet Laura. I'm sure she might feel like using that once in a while." Josh answered her.

"You're a jerk Josh. Why would I use some fucking dildos when I got the real thing on my bed, Come on. Do I have to beg you just so you can fuck me?" She was getting tired of his refusal.

"Okay. We'll do what you want but then I got to sleep after that and you won't try to wake me up until I get up by myself - you promise?" Josh said as he dragged her away from on top of his stomach where she had been sitting to pull off his clothes.

"I cross my heart and hope to die Josh." She jumped up as she made the cross with her hand on her chest. "I'll get that for you." She rushed to say as she went with her hands down on the buckle on his belt.

Josh smiled as she went to work on his trouser. It was always nice to have Latifah in desperation to get something; she would do almost anything to get it. "Okay, we are done." She said and stood up. He had removed his shirt and all that was left was to strip off his brief and get Latifah out of the flimsy gown she was wearing. She would most probably be naked under the gown as she always was anytime she was in the house.

He could see her nipple peeking out of the gown she was wearing. She was definitely horny - and if she was not before, well right now she was sure as hell already dripping. He pulled the gown off her through her head. Her rigid breast was carrying the hard strong nipple carefully so that he had to caress them with extreme care. She was definitely in need of some good banging that night because as soon as he touched her, she shuddered all over. He had to be gentle but exciting with her. He didn't want her making too much noise to disturb any of her roommates. He didn't spend too much time on foreplay but he made sure that he calmed down her nerves with kisses before penetrating her.

She stiffened a bit as he let his rod of pleasure thrust into her pot but soon she relaxed. She let him take good care of her and didn't make as much noise as she used to. She had transformed from the nuisance who was very chatty to a gentle puppy being led to death by its owner within few minutes - that was how much effect a dick had on her

About an hour after she walked into the bedroom, she was satisfied with the day. She had a nice time with friends and at the end of the day; she had something even better for dessert. She fell asleep in the arms of Josh who was also overtly tired. He could not have refused her request despite how sapped he was from the day's activities

- he had to always make sure that she was satisfied.

Chapter Six

The whole house was woken up by a continuous loud bang on the door of the house. Everyone ran out of the room towards the living room to see what was happening. The time was already past seven so they didn't fear that it could be thieves or any other person who could harm them.

"It's gotta be a neighbor that needs help urgently." Christine, Laura's girlfriend suggested.

"Well, it could be. But we don't have much neighbors that we make conversation with, and the one that we've had a conversation with - although I wouldn't call what we had a conversation, would be too proud to come to us if she happens to have any problem." Juanita answered.

"But we cannot stay here all day and not see who's knocking on the door. It might be some emergency stuff." Josh buttressed Christine's point.

"I guess we should open it then." Latifah said and they all nodded their agreement.

Juanita's boyfriend, Marcel was the one who went to open the door. He turned back to look at them after he opened the door and saw who was there. "I think it is one of your neighbors." He announced and he backed away from the door.

"Oh Fuck!" Latifah and Juanita murmured when they saw Ellen Marshall walk into their house. They knew that she was only going to bring trouble and that was one thing they didn't want at the moment. Laura was the one who stood up to face her when she locked the door after entering into the living room.

"How can we help you Mrs. Marshall?" Laura asked the woman.

"If you ladies want to help me, then I think y'all should start packing your bags and leave this country right away and never think of coming back. That's the only thing any of you can do for me that I cannot do for myself." Ellen answered.

"Who da fuck is this bitch?" Christine shouted. "She just ain't gon' walk into people's house and rant 'bout shit that don't make no sense. What your problem bitch?" she was going to approach her but Laura held her back.

"Well, ma'am. We don't know what diss you got with us but we don't think you're being reasonable here." Laura started. "We been neighbors for more than a year now and in all those times, neither me nor my friends have done nothing that could have got you pissed so we don't know what's causing these problems. Have we done something to ya that we don't realize? It's just gonna be better for you to tell us. That way we can sort everything out amicably --- you know - no need to shout..."

"So you want to know what problem I got with you bitches? You ladies haven't figured that out yet?" Ellen kept shouting. "Can't you see that everything in this room is what is wrong with the world?" she gestured at all of them and they looked around at each other for a moment to get what she was trying to say.

"So none of you still sees it? Uh? Is that how bad our society has lost values?" she yelled at them. "When we've all got our countries and we can't decide that we should stay there. We would rather impose on others and don't give shit about what's happening to our roots. Or do you give a fuck?" she turned to face Juanita and Latifah. "Yeah. Imma talking 'bout you two." She glazed her eyes at them.

"If there was no one like me making sure that your kind don't get into this country too much, I don't know where America's gonna be today. Your people just think we are running an amusement park here right? All they dream of everyday is to get into America. Well, let them know when you get back there that there ain't gon' be no entry again - zilch."

"Well ma'am. It seems the problem here is you. You're the one who has a problem with the way the society is working. Your view of life seems to be quite condescending and you look like you have problem with relating with what the world has become. It's not th----" Marcel was giving a reply to her outburst but Ellen couldn't wait for him to be done.

"You see boy," Ellen started. "It is blacks like you who are the problem with the African American race. You think everything's just gonna be okay with the world! You don't have to do shit, just make sure that everyone talks about their problems, air it out to the world and then you sit and wait for the government to solve that problem for you." She rolled her eyes at him and then continued. "I wouldn't be so surprised if your mother raised you on welfare - it's just that way with a lot of blacks. So if I'm talking to these foreigners in our country, I don't want you interrupting cos I got your faults at the back of my hands too." She hissed and turned back to Latifah and Juanita who had both accepted their situation for that morning.

"I'm gonna make life hell for the both of you cos the only thing you've added to this country has been population, your life means shit to no one and imma make sure that you get sent back to your people - go and learn how to make your own country better." She ended her attack on them, looked around and settled her eyes on Laura.

"You got something to say 'bout me?" Laura made faces at her.

"Oh yeah! I do." She answered and moved towards her. "But I'm gonna let you still be strong mentally to help your friends recover from this moment of truth." She looked at them all once again, gave a long hiss and walked out of the house. "Hope you feel better?" The college students heard a voice that sounded like her husband ask her.

"You guys got one hell of a neighbor." Josh commented few seconds after Ellen left.

"That was super fucked up. Is that what you bitches deal with every day?" Christine asked.

"No, not every day but we get stuffs close to that. She just yells at us from a distance most times. But it seems something got to her yesterday." Juanita answered.

"Maybe it was because of the party yesterday. But we didn't make that much noise - in fact, we didn't make any fucking noise." Marcel commented.

"I think it's just a 'her' problem. You guys heard what her husband asked her when she got outside?" Laura chipped in. "It's like she was dealing with something and lashing out was the way she could overcome it. Maybe she's gonna leave us be now." She added.

"I doubt if that bitch has said all she needed to say. You guys saw the way she looked at Laura?" Christine said. "If I'm still here and she comes here to make some fucking noise, imma put a punch in her ugly black face. Y'all should just go talk to her husband to make sure his bitch doesn't come here again."

"I don't think she's going to have any business coming here for a long time. But you guys can report her for harassment - she cannot just come and do all that shit and still walk away free." Josh suggested.

"She's a mother Josh. We don't want her kids thinking that their mother is deranged or something." Laura countered his suggestion.

"Well, I think she's deranged though. Cos no normal human being would behave the way she did." Josh didn't relent on making his point. "And she might just turn around one day and start lashing out her kids. You would be doing them a favor."

"Well, they've got a father and he should know to put his kids first if his wife begins to get crazy." Laura argued.

"You mean that man that just followed her and waited for her to be done with us? I don't think that guy gives a shit about anybody but his wife. They would both be dangerous to their kids." Josh smiled at her.

"You guys should not turn this into a joke." Christine yelled at Laura and Josh who were already laughing at the idea of how they could keep the discussion going.

"Maybe we should just leave then. There are better houses in better neighborhoods." Juanita said.

"No way. No fucking way..." they all bellowed at Juanita's idea.

"Then that fucking woman would have won. If anyone's gonna leave this place before we're done with college, it would have to be her - definitely not going to be us." Latifah spoke since Ellen left.

"I told you guys what to do already. If you don't report her, she's definitely gonna come back to do more. You can either make her stop now or she's gonna force you guys hands to do shit you wouldn't wanna do." Josh spoke up again.

"She can't do shit to us. She can only talk shit and threaten shit - but to do, she ain't got that power or balls to do them. If she wants to send either Juanita or Latifah outta the country, what she gonna use as their crime? They done no crime in their life and it's not like they can deport them just because one fucking agent says they should so it's never gonna stand in any court. She would only talk 'bout how she could have gotten us - but that's all she's gonna be able to do, talk." Laura answered seriously. "And me, I don't give a fuck what she wants to say about me. Her opinion of me means shit to everyone. What does she know - some tight assed 70's bitch tryna make me shake like a rat in a bag of nuts."

"Well. The shit has happened this morning and we should be expecting it again. But can we get to do other stuffs today? I'm getting bored of this talk already." Christine said.

"Yeah. I kinda woke up horny this morning. Maybe we can have a groupie - it's gonna be nice." Laura answered.

"Or you can just fucking say that you want a dick to fuck you. I'm sure that Latifah won't mind letting me do the honors if Christine would agree to it." Josh smiled at Laura who smirked.

"If you wanna fuck my girl you can ask Josh. I've told you this countless times, I'm not some stingy bitch. I know how to share the things that are so dear to me." Christine answered.

"So we good then!" Josh yelled.

"I never said we're good to go Josh." Latifah intervened.

"Come on Tipha. It's going to be nice. Or have you girls never had a threesome before?" Josh asked.

"I think we've done that like twice or three times." Juanita answered.

"So what's the big deal with this one then. We can just have sex instead of breakfast, and then we can have brunch later on in the day." Josh suggested.

"Alright. I'll do it but then we both gonna have to leave early to my room." Latifah agreed.

"I'm cool with that." Josh said and was already removing his clothes.

"Hey bro, calm down. I never said I was cool with what you suggested." Marcel spoke up.

"What the fuck!" Juanita yelled. "How are you not cool with that? You've done worse remember?"

"I know. But I'm just not really in the mood this morning." He said.

Christine walked over to where he was, grabbed his penis, and tugged at it. "If you get a head, will you be in the mood? You cannot chicken out on us. We're all going to do this."

"I might just change my mind but I never can be sure." Marcel smiled.

"You're a whore Marcel." Juanita laughed. You could have just said you wanted to be the first to go.

"Where's the fun in that?" Marcel asked as Christine unzipped his trousers. "You guys have to watch her till she's done then we all can now proceed to the main course." He stiffened when Christine's lips made contact with the skin of his dildo.

"We're just going to sit here and wait for you, you can be sure of that." Juanita replied sarcastically as she walked to Josh and began working on him too. Latifah was left with Laura so she also went down on her, all of them sucking and licking each other till they were all hot and ready to move on to the next.

They were all half clothed when they decided to change partners and they remained that way, exploring each other's lower half. Christine was the first to make a noise of pleasure so they all gathered round her to work, each person taking where they knew how to beat.

Chapter Seven

"Oh no!.... Yeah!" Latifah cried as Josh pumped all of his energy into pleasuring her. "Just fuck me till I die." She yelled over and over again. Her breast dancing and beating against her chest as the sway of their sensual activity kept her shaking all through. "Bang me... Fuck me..." she kept yelling.

Josh who had not participated with all of his energy in their threesome-like sexual act and still had the energy to satisfy his girlfriend who would not be satiated easily. He had been hitting her hard for the past fifteen minutes and she wasn't looking like she was going to cum any soon. He had been controlling himself not to release and he was not sure he would be able to hold for more than few minutes more. If he tried to make things easy for himself so that he could stay longer, she would not want to have any of that, and if he releases without her cumin, then he wouldn't sleep. The only thing he could do was try to see if she would let him suck her pussy. She was not really into shits like that, she loved to have it hard inside her, and she could ride it for a very long time, if the time was available.

"Oh my God! I'm gonna come now." She yelled as she used her hands to steady Josh's buttocks so that he could keep thrusting. "Ohh - oh—ooohh." Her breathe had seized as she waited for that rush of ecstasy to engulf her. "Yeaaahh—yeah --- ohhhhh!" she exclaimed when it finally overwhelmed her.

Josh rolled away from her, he had managed to keep himself till when she came before he released. If things hadn't turned out the way they had, he was not sure if he would have been able to go for five more minutes. "Your pussy is really something Tipha." He commented when he finally calmed down.

"So now you're going to commend my pussy for that huge favor I did for you - not me?" she smiled at him.

"Well, it's your pussy. If it gets anything, you get it too." Josh answered to set himself free from her hassling. "But you made a lot of noise. Everyone would be so teasing you with that today."

"Well, now they know how bad you can fuck. I'm sure no other pussy can stand what you gave me today." She eyed him as she slid under the quilt.

"You got something special under there babe. No one can battle that with you." Josh commented and jumped into bed with her.

"Maybe we can go another round now. You know I'm always up for a good time."

Latifah was already moving towards him under the sheets. "I've got nothing against that." She said and stretched her hands to grab his dick.

"What the fuck Tipha. You still want me to fuck you after all what I did just now?" he stared at her as though he was surprised. "I'm dry right now and I need to get my bearings right." He shook his head and turned away from her.

"Oh Fuck!" Latifah cursed silently as she remained in bed next to him.

"So you think they're gonna take it serious?" Ellen Marshal asked her husband after they got into their house.

"I really don't know - but you said a lot to them in there. I'm sure that if they don't leave, then they would also be ready to cause trouble." Roy answered.

"No matter the decision they decide to take, imma make sure that it favors my goal. Those bitches got to leave. They are just some bunch of dirty things that wants to infect our nation with their filthiness. If I can help it then they wouldn't get that chance." Ellen replied and sat down.

"I've been somewhat lenient with the way I handle immigrants. If they think that I was a bitch then, I wonder what they will think of me when I don't give a fuck about them anymore - when none of them gets into this country anymore as long as it gets through me." Her chest puffed out as she spoke.

"And those little nigga bitches - they've just been infected with the same mentality their whore mothers carried all their lives. They just think that talking about how shitty their lives have been and reminding everyone of how they were treated back in the days, they think that would beg the pity of others." She paused to look at her husband who was keenly listening to her rants. "And that black bitch - she thinks that her lesbian ass is going anywhere - she's just gonna end up in the deepest part of hell. She thinks that she's cool or something. She doesn't know that she's only digging a pit for herself."

"It's okay babe." Roy said to pacify her. "Let them just try to do something stupid and we'll be on them in no time."

"Whatever," Ellen said and kept quiet. She was fuming within her. She wished that she could just throw her neighbors out of the house and her country. She hated seeing Mexicans, Middle Easterners, or other refugees from other nations in her country. She always feels like they are the only reason why there's never been a good government since George W. Bush. She didn't have so much hate for Obama but she wasn't a lover of democrats either so she would never accept whatever he did as good and beneficial. What consoled her was the fact that Donald Trump was running for the presidency. She knew that people had formed an opinion on him, but she was certain that wouldn't matter when the Election Day came. The moment Trump is announced as the 45th President she would get to work. If her neighbors decide to play it cool with her, by that time, she was sure she would be able to do what she wants with them. With Trump's agenda rolling around purging America of its immigrant population, she was certain that her actions would be welcome if not lauded.

"I'm going to take a nap Roy." She said when she snapped out of her thoughts. She wasn't going to relent on making life hell for her neighbors.

"Alright. I'll join you as soon as I'm done with this pitch." He answered her without taking his eyes off his laptop.

Chapter Eight

The house was full again, the kids bustling around, their noise reaching into every room in the house. Ellen Marshal had missed her kids but she was also glad that they got to be away from home for the first time in years.

"You didn't tell us that you would renovate the house dad." Tanya said to her father after they finished their tour of the whole house.

"We didn't actually plan it; it just felt like it would be nice to do it." Roy answered his daughter's question. School was scheduled to resume in a week and Ellen had gone to pick the kids from her mum's that afternoon.

"But you guys could have told us when it was about to start." She went on arguing.

"Tanya, it was just a little renovation, not a big deal. So just leave it be." Her father said, tired of having to explain to her that he was busy and he could not afford to be distracted every thirty minutes.

"It doesn't look that way though. It's like you guys did a complete makeover." Tanya commented. "And what you did to my room was fab, I totally love it - super comfy." She went on and would have continued if Roy didn't stop her.

"Tanya," he started. "You can see that I'm super busy right now. You are distracting me and I can't get anything done if you keep up with that." He complained.

"Well. I didn't mean to disturb you dad. I've just kinda missed you a lot. That's all." Tanya answered apologetically.

"I missed you guys too but I've got to finish what I'm doing, then we can have a good time together." Roy said, not looking at the fake face his daughter was making. She used that face to make him agree with whatever she wanted when she was still little but he had learnt not to always make it work. "Go and play with your brothers for now. Or you guys could just go disturb your mum a little bit. She's been buried in work all summer." He suggested.

"Of course. Like you weren't buried in work also." Tanya commented and ran away to look for her siblings.

It had been just he and his wife in the house all summer. They were able to get the peace they used to have after they got married. But once they started having children two years into their marriage, everything had changed. First, it was something they could manage - just Tanya making trouble for them but then David came along and things got harder. They both had a career they were trying to build and adding the stress of raising two kids to it, they were defeated. Roy had to reduce his presence in his office and thanks to the understanding partners he had, there were no repercussions on his finances. He had helped with raising the kids for a year and the next year, they got a nanny to help them with the job. He was able to go back to work and some years after that, they had a set of twins. Now that they were all grown up - maybe somewhat, he had expected that the trouble they would cause him would be reduced but it seemed like it only gets worse. Most nights, he had to wrestle the twins off his neck whenever they try to play with him. He knew that if he ignored them, then they wouldn't be happy with him so he always leaves whatever he is doing at that moment and take his time to make them happy till they fall asleep. But Tanya was not a baby anymore and she understood what working meant. If he fails to look over every pitch that is brought to him, he might just begin to sink the company into a deep pit. All these was still going on in his mind when he heard Ellen yell at someone.

“You should go to your room now and stay there till I tell you to come outside.” It seemed to be Tanya that she was yelling at. Roy stood up from his laptop and walked towards their room. He met Tanya walking back to her room with tears on her face. He tried to stop her but she wouldn’t wait.

"Hey. What happened?" he asked Ellen as soon as he walked into the bedroom.

"Can you imagine that girl telling me that she wants to go for Hillary's campaign that is coming up soon? She has the gut to mention that name in this house?" Ellen yelled.

"Hey calm down baby. You shouldn't take it so hard on Tanya. She does not know anything yet so it could just be her friends that have convinced her to come. We would make her see that the democrats are not people to relate with and she would see reason with us. But we cannot go around making our daughter cry – we cannot do that." Roy reprimanded his wife.

"Alright. Maybe I overreacted. But why would she choose to go for Hillary's campaign when she know that we are republicans in this house? That's what's shocking to me." Ellen answered.

"We'll figure this out Ellen. You don't have to worry about that. We are her parents and we would make sure that she sees the reason why we make the decisions that we do."

"Okay. I'll go talk to her then." Ellen said and dropped the files she was working on.

"We'll go together." Roy added and walked with her towards Tanya's room.

"Tanya honey." Ellen called out to her daughter before she opened the door. Tanya had her back turned towards the door and she didn't turn around when her parents came into her room.

"Hey honey," her mother called her again, this time, stretching her hand to touch her gently on the shoulder. She shrugged her mother's hand off and sat up on the bed.

"Hey Tanya," Roy intervened in the situation. "Your momma is sorry for the way she reacted when you told her of what you wanted to do. She's really sorry."

"And what about you dad?" Tanya asked, "Do you now have time to talk to me?"

"Come on baby. You don't go on being like that. I would always have time for you and your siblings. You guys are my top priority but I just had to finish looking at that pitch today. I was planning on coming to chill with you all." Roy explained his action. "And I'm sorry that you feel as if I don't care for you. I love you Tanya." He smiled at her and she smiled back.

"Okay," Tanya agreed.

"Good," Ellen came back into the discussion. "But we have to talk about what you told me Tanya." She added and when her daughter didn't make any move to show that she was against talking, she went on.

"Why do you want to go for rally?" she asked and waited patiently for the answer she was going to get.

"I think Hillary Clinton is cool. She really cares for people and I think that kind of a person should be the president." Tanya answered.

"And what has she done that you think makes her cool? Do you know of anyone?"

"Well, I heard that she's always making donations to help people with their study stuffs and the likes and that she's even planning on giving scholarships to student-parent so that they can get a balance between going to school and raising a child." Tanya said, staring at her mother who didn't seem to care for any of the things she just said. "And I've heard a whole lot more of the things she does about human rights, gay rights, I think she's just cool." Tanya finished and waited for either of her parents to reply.

Ellen did first. She would have come out all strong and brutal but she realized that it was her daughter she was dealing with and she would not want to lose her to the other side just because she just couldn't calm herself down to explain how things work to her. "You see Tanya; I cannot say that Hillary didn't do what you said she did. She did them but so does a lot of people too - in their own way." Ellen started. "But I want you to take it from me that everything you see and hear is not what it seems."

"What you see Hillary Clinton doing is what Obama is doing also. They know what the public wants to hear and that is what they are going to say to make sure that you fall in love with their person - you will never know who they really are. They say one thing in front of the television and then they go back to do something else. Or do you think that the war in the Middle East is just between the countries there?" she paused to let her daughter think for a while.

"No! And before you begin to think that America has been helping to get those countries to stop killing each other, America is one of the reasons why there is still war going on in those places and it is also a fact that the number of civilian death increases whenever there is intervention from external military bodies - and this is what the United States majors on." Ellen finished her point. "Do you see that those whom you say that care for what happens to others and fight for the rights of other humans, try to bring peace into other people's land, are the ones who are making things unbearable for the citizens of those countries. The Unites States is the reason why there are so many refugees."

"But how can that be...." Tanya asked, confused. She didn't know what to think anymore.

"It is very simple Tanya. These democrats come out to tell you about how they would go over to countries like Syria, Iran, Pakistan,

Afghanistan and the likes and use their military to stop the war, to protect the civilians, yet there are laws and bills been passed every day to favor companies that produce the guns that the rebels in these countries use. All of these companies successes will add to the economy of this nation and everyone at the top is fine with that."

"They can act as the ones trying to bring peace to a place and at the same time, they would support to arm their opponent just so that they can make profit off of them. Is that the kind of government that you want?" she asked her.

"Trump may not be the most lovable person in the whole world but one thing I know is that he says what is true. He doesn't need to lie to you to be able to get you to love him - he doesn't care if you love him or not. All he cares about is making sure that everyone knows where they stand."

"He is not going to tell you that he is going to start a program where you can get what you want and pay as it will be convenient for you. He would do that and tell you that you would have to pay him forever for everything you buy. He would let you know what you would gain from doing one thing or the other and what could be detrimental to you if you decide to follow his dreams."

"He will tell you the truth about your life and make you see the facts that are staring at you right in the face. So I don't understand when people try to convince you to follow an assumption when there is fact staring at you right in the face - Trump is the truth that you are seeing." Ellen said and rested.

"I didn't know that you were this passionate about Trump mum." Tanya commented after listening to her mother sing praises of Trump.

"Now Tanya, don't get me wrong. I know that Trump would be the right choice for us but all what I just said is not just for Donald Trump, it is for every Republican out there. We see life as it is. We don't lie to people about what they can get from their efforts and we don't let people think that we are okay with them shitting on us when we are not. That's what Republicans stand for and that's what Trump stands for and that's why I know that he is the one you should be dying to see in the white house next." Ellen cleared her daughter's doubt.

"I think I have a new perspective about politics now mom." Tanya smiled at her mother who patted her on the hand and smiled back.

"Well, it is good that you have all the information available and make your choice. It wouldn't be good for you to just pick one because it is the only thing you know." Ellen said. "And before I forget, who told you about Hillary Clinton?" Ellen asked her.

"You don't have to worry about that anymore momma. I don't think I'm going for that rally again." Tanya answered, trying not to answer the question.

"Hey Tanya. I'm going to worry about this so just do us all a favor and tell me who invited you to that rally." Ellen wouldn't let her daughter convince her that easily that everything was alright.

"It was Laura." Tanya answered reluctantly.

"Which of the Laura's? The neighbors?" Ellen asked, raising her hips off the bed already, ready to march out of her house to the house where Laura and her friends were staying.

"Laura at the other side of our house." Tanya said. She knew that she had put Laura in a big mess, but she could not lie to her mother without her mother knowing and that would have been unnecessary in the end.

Ellen was almost barging out of the room when Roy caught her and pulled her back into the room. "We will talk about this before we both go over there. You cannot go there while you are still furious." He said and kept his hold on her arms firm.

"So Laura told you all those stuffs about Hillary Clinton?" her father asked to be sure of how he was going to react when he went with his wife to the other house.

"Yeah. I've not really had time to go online to read stuffs about her." Tanya replied.

"Okay. But I don't want you talking to that girl anymore - is that okay?" Roy warned his daughter.

"I don't see what's so bad about someone wanting me to share the same view as hers, isn't that what you and mum are trying to do also. Then why should I not talk to her again because of that?" Tanya was protesting but her father maintained his ground.

"I don't want you to talk to Laura again and that's it - no arguing about that." Roy said and pulled his wife alongside him and left Tanya alone in her room.

"Why didn't you let me leave when I was still furious with that bitch? I could have torn her apart for teaching my daughter shit." Ellen demanded when Roy dragged her into their bedroom.

"And what would have happened after that?" Roy glared at her. "You think this is just about you again? You do anyhow to those girls and they can sue you. You know that right?" Roy yelled at her and she calmed down a bit.

"But she has no right to be talking to my daughter about some stuffs that I don't approve of - she cannot do that." Ellen yelled out of desperation for something to say.

"It was not like she forced Tanya to do anything Ellen. Tanya chose to and there's nothing we can do about that but I will still go to her and let her know that I don't want her communicating with my daughter anymore. I will get her arrested if I see her say as much as a hi to any of my children." Roy declared.

"Well, I'm not letting you go alone. I have a piece of my mind to give to her too." Ellen added.

"Nope. You are not going Ellen. You would only go there to cause trouble and that is not what I am going there to do. I am going there to talk. Can you do that?" Roy asked her.

"You think I can't do that Roy? Come on. You know that I can keep my cool when I need to - I'm just going to have to do that now even though I would just prefer to tear her eyes out of her socket - the fucking girl with the lesbian ass."

"Okay. You will go there and you can say all you want but you cannot touch anyone of them. Is that okay?" Roy warned her before leading the way and the both of them left for their neighbor's house.

"You cannot come into my house and begin to yell at me. No! You guys can't do that." Laura was reacting to the action of Roy and Ellen Marshal in her house.

"You think you're shit right? Well, I don't care about that. All I want to warn you about is to stay away from my daughter. I don't want you to ever talk to her again and if I see you say as much as a hi to any of my children, I'll make sure that I get a restraining order against you." Roy made his intention known to her.

"Well, I'll stay away from your kids. What's my problem with that? You guys can fuck out of this house now and if I ever see you also step foot here, I'll make sure I get a similar restraining order issued to all your family member." Laura replied.

"Just one more thing." Ellen said when she got to the door of the apartment. "You had better change your ways because your sorry lessie ass is going to end up in the deepest part of hell if you keep offering it to fellow females like you. That is what you should be more concerned about, not how you will get more people to follow you in the chase for a fucking leader who would cut you all more slacks to indulge in your nonsensical acts when they won't be there to help you to deal with the repercussions."

"Hey bitch. Are you telling me that you're still so behind in the revolution of the society today that you think being a lesbian is a sin or something? Come on, try to be modern a bit or maybe you can pretend to be if you don't know how to be modern." Laura replied her.

"You can call me what you want. I'm sure that when the time comes, you would remember how someone who hates you so much gave you one important advice that could have saved you from the mess you got yourself in." Ellen responded and walked out of the house before things would get out of hand.

Chapter Nine

Ellen Marshall was in her office along Tyvola Drive when Maggie Holloway peered through the door. She didn't ask if she was busy or not. Instead, she just walked in and took her seat. Ellen stared at the woman with a facial expression that was asking *is there any trouble and what can I do for you.* When Maggie didn't make any move like she was going to leave or say anything, Ellen decided to talk first.

"What happened this time Maggie?"

"Nothing. I just feel like looking at you while you work." Maggie answered.

"There are lots of people out there that you can watch work - why do you have to come to my office to watch someone work?" Ellen looked at the woman with a confused eye.

"It's you I'm talking about Ellen. I like to watch you work." Maggie explained herself.

"Oh! Okay. I see." Ellen said and went back to work ignoring the woman in front of her. But that was not going to work for long because Maggie soon began to raise discussions that didn't interest her.

"Maggie, I'm kind of busy here and you are terribly distracting me." Ellen spoke up when she could no longer take it.

"Of course. You're busy." Maggie said and stood up to leave the office but she paused when she got to the door. "Is there any other black person working in this office apart from the both of us?" she turned and asked her question.

"I don't know of any other person." Ellen replied curtly.

"So why don't you want anything to do with me? You think you are too light to be considered a black woman or what?" Maggie demanded.

"I don't get you Maggie..." Ellen commented. She knew that a day like this was still going to come, when Maggie would no longer be able to keep pretending as if she didn't know that she was being ignored by the only one person she could call a sister at work.

"You know what I'm talking about Ellen." Maggie closed the door and walked back into the office. "You treat me like I'm shit - like you don't want to have anything to do with me. Like you are a better version of who I can never dream of becoming. You would say that is not how you treat me uh?" she posed with a ready-to-argue stance.

Ellen dropped all what she was doing and paid her attention to Maggie. There was no point not telling her the truth when it was obvious that she could figure it out already.

"You see Maggie, I had hoped that I would bond with you the first time you got to this office but then I realized something about you - you liked democrats, although you are not someone who is political. But you will still choose a democrat over a republican any day; I knew that we couldn't be friends. I can never be friends with you." Ellen confessed.

"I'm sure you could have said that all these while. Instead of letting me hang around every time - and looking like a fool. At least you owe that to humanity." Maggie said.

"I don't owe you anything Maggie. I just did what was okay by me. It was for you to figure out what was okay for you and if you hung around then it was because it was okay for you. I never tried to encourage you for once that I could interested in talking to you." Ellen said in defense.

"Of course. You never did that." Maggie didn't see any point talking about the situation any more so she stood up to leave. "But you wonder why I wouldn't go for a republican any time - this is an example of that reason." Maggie paused again at the door to add the last comment before she left.

It wasn't how Ellen had seen her day going but it wasn't that bad. She's had worse reactions from people who felt like she was treating them like shit. She's had countless of them that seeing Maggie blast was nothing to her, she just resumed her work and moved on. The election was only a few days away - she couldn't let someone fuck up her mood. She was seeing a win in front of her and she was going to get that win.

Chapter Ten

It was the evening of November 8 and Ellen Marshall was in the living room with her family watching the proceedings of the election - as the results were being displayed and the hopes for their future, glaring right at them in the face. There had been no work for her that day and right after voting she had remained indoors with her family. She was confident that her candidate would win and the only reason she was sitting, watching as the results were being sent in was so that she could see firsthand what it would be like after the results would be announced.

By the time it was past ten, she sent the children to sleep and stayed up with Roy waiting for the remaining results to come in.

The morning of November 9 was another great day in the life of Roy and Ellen Marshall. It marked the beginning of a new dawn in their life and story and it meant that Ellen was finally going to be able to execute her plans soon. She had been bidding her time, waiting for the elections, praying that it favors her and now that everything had worked out, she was definitely going to make every minute till when her plan would be put in place count. She was going to frustrate hell out of the lives of the girls who have been feeling untouchable for months now.

She had spent the whole night staying up and watching the victory count grow. Now, she was going to give herself a deserved rest but before then, she had a ceremonial sex she had planned with Roy. Then, she would sleep like a baby till the afternoon.

Roy was already naked and waiting for her in the bedroom when she walked in. She smiled at him and his huge dangling extension took on a little more rigidity in her presence. "You couldn't wait for me or what?" Ellen teased him as she locked the door so that the kids wouldn't bump in on them having a good time. She let them also celebrate the victory of Donald Trump in whatever way they can.

"I could wait but bobby felt like he had to drag in some cool air before he goes into the hot zone."

"Well, I'm sure that bobby would forget everything about cool air very soon." Ellen was teasing him as she also got out of her own clothes. Her large fresh supple breast with a dark nipple followed her as she moved towards her husband, her hands playing underneath her, in between her legs.

"You shouldn't be doing that by yourself when I'm here." Roy said and dragged her hands out from beneath her. He carried her to sit on the bed and sent his finger to work her freshly shaved clit. He rubbed on the surface, massaging the skin there methodically. Ellen only had to sit on the bed, and she busied herself with smacking her lips as she swam in the pleasure her husband was instigating in her. She basked in the aura of sensual bliss as it came to her.

Roy played a tough but soft game on her before penetrating her with his fingers, he was having her already expectant of the peak moment yet he was able to keep her to enjoy what she was having at hand. His hands worked swiftly making little pitter-patter noises as it went on.

"Are you going to make me full with just this? We ain't going to do the real thing?" Ellen forced herself to speak up from the intoxication of the hot sex.

"Okay, we'll move to the next thing." Roy said and removed his fingers but still kept on tapping her on the surface, just to keep her waiting for his huge twin to come for her. He rubbed his penis to make it fully erect then he guided it in its journey into the abyss of her hotspot. Like she was always did, she stiffened at the initial contact his skin made with hers but calmed down as he led his manhood into its first thrust into her total darkness. He began to ride her right where he was standing, his laps colliding with the mattress of their bed. There were in no rush to sleep or to leave for work – they had all the time in the world to please each other so he gave a very slow ride that dug into her entirety. She felt every pump of blood flowing through the veins of his penis as they worked her slowly – she felt the hotness of the blood and that pleased her even more.

She began to shudder about ten minutes into the game, feeling every inch of her nerves getting excited, her muscles jumping at the feel of the ecstasy to come and her mind managed to ride along with the bliss of the beautiful moment she was enjoying with her husband. Roy adjusted his position, he turned her over on the bed and climbed up with her, her knees on the bed and her arms in front of her - they were going doggy. He sent himself into her once again and this time, he wasn't going at a slow pace. He pushed into her fast and hard hitting the spot where she always loved to be stimulated. In no time, he already had her cursing silently, biting her teeth to make sure that she didn't shout when it becomes too much for her to handle. He took her on the new adventure and kept her in pure exhilaration all through the moment. When he finally began to slow down his pace, he sent his hands forward to rub on her clit and at a steady pace, he continued inserting himself into her, never letting her have a dull moment.

He took her next on a missionary journey when he turned her back to rest on the bed. He cupped her huge breasts in his hands and kept pummeling her with his big cock. Ellen kept herself steady by holding onto the frame of the bed. Her legs were beginning to get weak from the non-stop feeling of being high and her eyes were already shut. Roy carried her into cloud nine for some more time before they were both unable to keep up with delaying the huge burst of ecstasy they were waiting for. Like they had been practicing for it for years, they both came at the same time, with Roy falling on her as he was totally spent. They remained unmoving for some few more minutes before Roy moved away from atop her and they hugged each other as they fell asleep.

All things considered, it had been a perfect morning. The joy of having their presidential candidate go on to win the election despite all the odds against him and the spurt of pleasure that were able to keep having undisturbed after they heard the good news.

By the time they would wake up, it would be with a different attitude towards the world.

Chapter Eleven

Three weeks had passed since the election results were announced and everything was almost back to normal except for the protesters in the streets who were not ready to have Donald Trump as their next president. They were growing in number each day, coming out to show their dissatisfaction at the president elect of their country. With the huge number of people who had taken to the streets and those who were ranting all day on social media, one is left to wonder if they were not the same people who voted in Trump. Or how could it be so possible that a huge number of people are angry at the results of the election? What would be their claim? That the election was rigged? Or that they have back stabbing goons amidst themselves? Whatever their decision would be on that, Ellen Marshall didn't give a dam about it. Her choice president has won the election and he would make sure that things don't keep happening the same way they've been doing it for some time now.

She was closed from work for the day and she was on her way home to her family. For the past three weeks, she had been resuming to work with a smile on her face because she knew that she was finally at the edge of making sure little or no immigrants were allowed into her country to mess it up once again. She was in total support of the Great Wall of America - something to keep the Mexicans out of their country. They needed to be able to breathe fresh air without having to see some Mexicans in their sombrero walking along their streets. North Carolina had been one of the deciding states that helped the president-elect to steal an edge over Hillary and she would forever be joyous with the indwellers. All she had to do now was wait for Friday the 20th of January for the inauguration and she could switch to full mode - ready to take on any immigrant she encounters. The top on her list was definitely her neighbors. She knew that they would be already be expecting her but she had decided to make them feel like she's not unto them anymore. She wanted them to feel comfortable with not being hassled around and then suddenly, she would be on them again. Life was good for her and so it will remain till she got tired of it - if she ever will.

"Hey bitches. You ready to leave yet or not?" Latifah shouted at her roommates. They were already running late for a class. "You bitches should get your fucking ass out here now or I'm going to leave the both of you behind and you can take the bus when you're ready to leave." She kept yelling.

"Just be quiet already." Laura said as she came out of her room, all set to leave for school.

"We're like fifteen minutes late already. Before we drive to school, do you know how late we will be?" Latifah was not going to let them make her feel like she was getting worked up on nothing. "Hey Juanita. You better get your sorry ass out here." She shouted at the only person they were waiting for.

"Come on girl, you don't want me to wear panties to school today or what? Just chill and before you know it we will be in school already." She said as she fought to zip her jeans.

"Of course, we are some fucking magicians who would just shake off the cobweb from our brooms and zoom off to school." Latifah hissed. "Let's fucking be on our way already." She yelled at them and they filed out of the house.

Laura was locking the door when she heard Latifah curse again. "Will just stop saying that fucking word this morning. I've heard it too many times today already and it was all from you." She said battling with the lock only to turn around and rain down her own set of curse words. "How the fuck did this shit happen?" she yelled after getting the anger of her chest. She had calculated in her mind that they should be able to get to the lecture in the next fifteen minutes but that no longer seemed to be feasible.

"This car was fine when we went to sleep yesterday. All four tires cannot be deflated at a time, someone must have done this." Latifah said. "We still went out in this car yesterday night and it was all okay. That fucking bitch must have come to do this during the night." She said what was on her mind.

"I cannot think of anyone else who would do this. Or what reason would someone have to deflate all our tires when they are not trying to trap us in the house to steal or do any other shit to us. It must have been that modafucka." Laura said as she walked down to where her friends were standing, still shocked to see the car in the condition it was in.

I think that bitch has caught all the fun she needs. We shouldn't let her keep getting away with all the stunts she's pulling with us." Juanita commented.

"I guess we will have to start filming her again. We provoke her to do some very crazy shit to us and then we can catch her when she tries to retaliate." Latifah gave a suggestion.

"I guess that seems to work very well." Juanita agreed. "We got to be on our way to go wait for the bus though." She said reminding them that they had a class they were already late for.

"Of course." Laura said and they all walked towards the bus stop to wait for their ride to arrive.

Back in the summer not quite long after Ellen had come into their house to raise hell on them, they had gotten the idea of making videos of her whenever she attacks them. Up until that morning, her attacks had always been with her mouth, she had never raised a finger on them or their property but after that day she had resulted to violent means. They were glad that it was at that same time the idea of recording every incident they have with her.

The first one had been one of the best ones. It was a weekend and Laura was having sex with her boyfriend. The rest of them were in the living room, talking about the classes they were to have the next semester. Josh had run up to pick something in Latifah's room and he was on his way back when Ellen barged into their house. She had come with a baseball bat and began to hit several of their belongings, shattering them on the ground, trying to destroy the wall of their home. Josh had stayed back a bit and caught everything on camera. She had a murderous look in her eye that afternoon and looked like she would strangle anyone who tried to question what she was doing. Josh had remained hidden all through the shit and when she left, he came out and showed them what he had. They could sue her for what she did but they didn't think it was the right time. They wanted her to have done too many bad things that money would not be able to compensate - they wanted her to get to desperate of driving them out of town that she wouldn't mind becoming a criminal in the process. From that first time, they had started achieving their goal because few days after that, they had another incident with her.

Laura was on the lawn talking to someone on the phone. She had been super active all morning so her adrenaline was still running high and she was somewhat shouting while making the call. Few months after they arrived at the neighborhood, Ellen Marshall had approached them about joining her Republican campaign. They had told her then that there were liberals and they were not going to make a move to antagonize what they believe in. She had been pissed back then and that seemed to have been the start of their troubled relationship with her. On that particular less-sunny summer afternoon, Laura had been talking to someone about politics and then she had shouted, "Tanya, forget about what your mum thinks. You have to be able to make decisions for yourself. It is those decisions that would..." she was still saying this when Ellen Marshall got to her front. Unbeknownst to Laura, Ellen had been in front of her house, about to get into her car to go out when she overheard what Laura was saying.

"What can I do for you Ellen?" Laura had asked after she excused herself from the call and ended it.

"I would like to know which Tanya you were talking to if you don't mind." Ellen answered.

"Well, I kind of mind. I can talk to whomever I want to and you don't have the right, not even the privilege to ask me that kind of a question. You can leave for wherever you were headed." Laura hissed and started pressing her phone.

"Laura, I am trying to be civilized here and that's the only reason why I am asking you the question." Ellen spoke up. "I would prefer you tell me if it was Tanya my daughter you were speaking to or not. For your own sake." She threatened.

"What if it were your daughter? What 'r you gonna do? Threaten me with what?" Laura yelled at her.

"You just say that it was my daughter and you would know exactly what it is that I would do to you." Ellen smiled at Laura who seemed not to be rattled by the woman's threat.

"If you would like to know so much then, yes, it was your daughter Tanya that I was speaking to." Laura raised her smartphone up for Ellen to see. "You can see that those are her digits right?" she smiled back at the woman who was no longer smiling and like the flash of a lightning, her punch had hit Laura squarely in the chin and it sent her sprawling to the ground.

Latifah who had started watching the scene from when they were arguing had also caught everything on camera. They had two tapes of her assaulting them within four days but they were not okay with just that, they needed her to go way over the edge and then they would have everything they need to take her down. They would have gotten it all - apart from the little brawl they had here and there if her husband had not intervened in the matter. He had banned her from going to their neighbors' house and he was not to talk to them. He had also gone to warn the college girls that he didn't want any trouble with anyone so they should not try to incite his wife to be angry. They were not happy about that development but since it would keep the crazy bitch off their back, they were happy to agree to it. And cool were things until summer was over and their kids came. But then also, what they had was only a heated conversation.

Chapter Twelve

Ellen Marshall was driving into her street around six thirty in the evening. She was still feeling very good inside with all she had been able to achieve that day - the most exciting one being deflating all the tires to the car of her college student neighbors. And it was with this joy, smile that she parked her car, and waved to the girls who were sitting outside of their home.

When she saw the girls walking towards her, she knew that her plan had worked. She had pissed them off and now they were going to do something that would hasten their deportation when the time comes. "How you girls doing today?" she asked them as though she cared for their answer.

"Hey Ellen. We are not here to talk to you about our day." Laura replied her.

"Oh! I see. So to what do I owe this pleasure of having you on my property?" she smiled wickedly at them.

"We know you are the one who messed with our car. There's no one else who can do something as stupid as that." Laura answered her question.

"Well, if you know that I am the one, then why don't you guys just already report me to the cops and get me arrested. Or are you afraid they would pay you no attention?" she laughed at them but they kept looking at her with a straight face.

"We don't need the cops to take care of our shit for us when we can take care of it by ourselves." Latifah responded.

"So you bitches think that you can beat me out here in the open and get away with it? Even if you drag me to somewhere that is confined and do whatever you want to me, you can never get away with it. You guys are just so dumb." She laughed at them.

They smiled for the first time since accosting her. "Why the fuck do you think we are going to beat you or any of those shit to you? You think we are like you. Who's got no control over her fucking head? You're going crazy. If you haven't realized that yet then we are telling you." Juanita spoke up.

"So what are you guys doing here then? Uh?" Ellen asked them, confused about the situation. It was not what she had planned that was going to happen.

"We just thought that it would be nice for you to know that you would never be giving us any trouble again. Not ever in your life." Laura announced.

"Now, why would I do that? When all I have to do is wait till January 20 to throw you guys out of this neighborhood." Ellen commented.

"You see Ellen, if you try to make any move against us any time before or after January 20, then you can be sure that you wouldn't have a job." Laura answered her back and moved closer. She brought out her phone, scrolled to her videos and played it for Ellen to see.

"You can see yourself there right? Messing around with our house, destroying everything that was standing. Well, that one isn't as good as the one we recorded for the day you hit me. I'm sure that you'll be able to explain what happened but when we show them other videos of you threatening us with deportation because you are in a position to make it happen, I'm sure your explanation would be shit to your superiors. And if they don't do anything to you, then you can be sure of these videos going viral. Whichever way, you're going to have to let us be as from now on." Laura moved closer to her to show that they were not intimidated by her position any longer.

"Well, I can leave you guys alone but then you just made things worse for your people who would have dreams of coming into America because I will make sure that every request that passes through me gets denied and that can be quite much because I get up to hundreds of paper seeking for refuge in this great country. I can give up the fight with you two to focus on that single goal." Ellen said to Latifah and Juanita. "And as for you Laura. I know you still think you are being cool with all your gay shits but then let me just remind you that you ain't shit to no one. And when you die, your gay ass is going end up in hell." She said with disdain in her face for the lesbian.

"Oh! Yeah! I know that I'm gonna rot in hell like a whole lot of other people but who gives a damn. I am going to be with my fellow gays and we can continue the party over there." Laura replied her. "All I need to tell you

Ellen is that you've got to learn how to loosen up a bit. Life is not always about what has been, it has a lot to do with what is and what would be and if you can see this, I am sure that you would be able to accept people for who they are and you'll see that your conservative beliefs would only give you shit for the rest of your lives."

"Thanks for the advice Laura. But I think I like my life and the people I care about just the way everything is." Ellen said and walked away from them towards her family who had been staring out the window at the little altercation.

Laura, Juanita and Latifah also walked back to their house, satisfied that they were finally able to get the woman off their back without having to hurt her family.

She was disappointed in herself that some little girls beat her but then, she lived to fight another day and other pressing causes. Ellen Marshall would wait her time and in the meantime, she would make life miserable for other immigrants that cross her way and every other poverty-stricken black citizen of the nation. She would rid her great nation of those pests that are slowly eating at it from the inside - she would strip them of their strength and leave them open to despair till they will have no choice but to return to their motherland.

the end

Made in the USA
Columbia, SC
07 November 2017